# BOOM BOOM CRASH!!!

Marie Barbee

AuthorHouse™
1663 Liberty Drive
Bloomington, IN 47403
www.authorhouse.com
Phone: 1 (800) 839-8640

Published by AuthorHouse 11/27/2019

ISBN: 978-1-7283-1561-4 (sc)
ISBN: 978-1-7283-1560-7 (e)

Library of Congress Control Number: 2019907577

Printed in the United States of America.

authorHOUSE®

Long long ago, deep in the forest, there is a tiny little town.

Every night when the sun goes down and the moon comes up, the people of the town can hear the soft, faint sound "BOOM BOOM CRASH, BOOM BOOM CRASH."

As the townsfolk are scared and frightened of the sound "BOOM BOOM CRASH, BOOM BOOM CRASH", they start gathering in the town square. Mrs. Smith says, "We should not be afraid of the sound and go find out what it is."

The town gathered their lanterns and walking sticks and started down the long dirt road. They could hear the soft, faint sound of "BOOM BOOM CRASH, BOOM BOOM CRASH" getting louder and louder.

At the end of the long dirt road was an old wooden house where the sound "BOOM BOOM CRASH, BOOM BOOM CRASH" was coming from.

Mrs. Smith knocks on the front door, but nobody answers. As she creaks open the old wooden door, they could hear the sound "BOOM BOOM CRASH, BOOM BOOM CRASH" coming from inside.

As they entered the house, Mrs. Smith calls out "Is anybody there?" but nobody answered. They could see a chair, couch, and a TV set.

They walk through a swivel door into the next room and could hear "DRIP DROP DRIP DROP" coming from the sink faucet but nobody was there.

As they entered the next room, they could hear the soft faint sound of whistling. They realized that the sound was coming from the curtain blowing in and out of the open window.

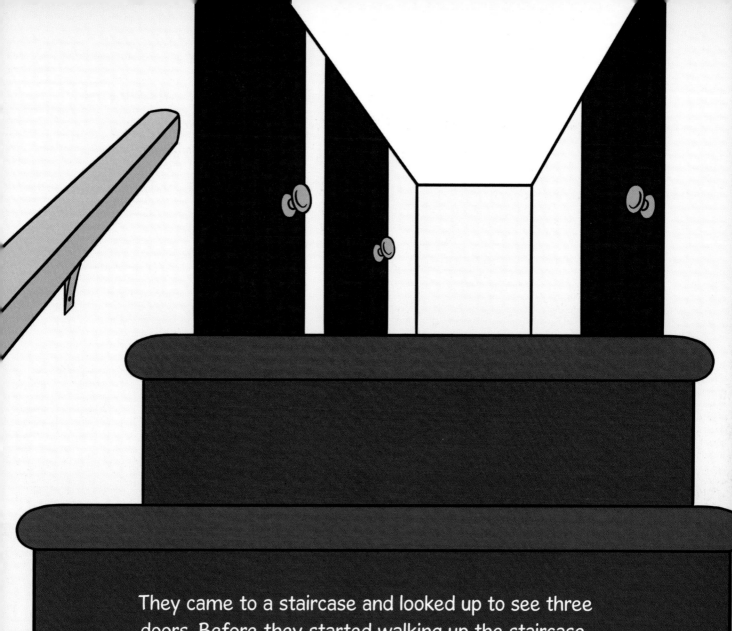

They came to a staircase and looked up to see three doors. Before they started walking up the staircase, the sound "BOOM BOOM CRASH, BOOM BOOM CRASH" was coming from one of the rooms.

As they walked up the stairs, they could hear and feel the stairs creak and crack underneath their feet.

As they opened the first door, no one was inside but old dusty moving boxes.

As they creaked open the second door,
they entered an empty room.

As they started to walk to the third door, they could hear "BOOM BOOM CRASH, BOOM BOOM CRASH" getting louder and louder. They pushed the door open slowly and looked inside.

As Mrs. Smith opens the door, she says
"Hello, is anyone there?" A monkey
appears from behind the boxes.

Mrs. Smith asks, "Who are you?" "My name is Timmy and
my family forgot me when they moved away." "At night, I
get scared and lonely. Playing the drums makes me happy."
"Your music is so nice. Would you like to come live with
me and play your drums for the family's in our town."

"Yes! I would love to come live with you," Timmy gets so excited that he plays his drums for Mrs. Smith. The townspeople pick up Timmy and the drum set and carry them back to town.

Every day, when Mrs. Smith would sell her flowers, Timmy would play his drums for the families in the town, Timmy now had a family and somewhere to belong and he was happy again.